VERY UNCUTE!

This ∧ book belongs to...

_____

_____

_____

I'm Not Cute, I'm Dangerous

An original concept by author Bruna De Luca
© Bruna De Luca
Illustrated by Benedetta Capriotti

First Published in the UK in 2021 by
MAVERICK ARTS PUBLISHING LTD

Studio 11, City Business Centre, 6 Brighton Road,
Horsham, West Sussex, RH13 5BB
© Maverick Arts Publishing Limited 2021
+44 (0)1403 256941

American edition published in 2021 by Maverick Arts Publishing,
distributed in the United States and Canada by Lerner Publishing
Group Inc., 241 First Avenue North, Minneapolis, MN 55401 USA

ISBN 978-1-84886-706-2

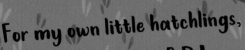

I'm Not Cute, I'M DANGEROUS

Written by
Bruna De Luca

Illustrated by
Benedetta Capriotti

"She's going to be a real **fireball!**" boasted Mom and Dad.

But Fifi was more of a...

...furball.

"She's not a **proper** crocodile. She's **cute!**" her sisters smirked.

"Cutesy wootsy!"

"Cuddly wuddly!"

"Coochie coochie coo!"

"I am NOT cute.
I'm DANGEROUS!"

Fifi snapped.

"It's not fair," she said.

"I sharpen my teeth **twice** a day...

...and practice my **sneaking**.

But all they see is this **fluff**."

Then Fifi had a brilliant idea.

"I know! I can be spiky..."

...dangerously spiky!"

And she was, until...

...a rain shower made her plan fall flat.

And a warm breeze **fluffed** it up completely.

"Nice hairdo, sis!"

"Cutesy wootsy!"

"Cuddly wuddly!"

"Coochie coochie coo!"

"I am NOT cute. I'm DANGEROUS!" Fifi snapped.

Fifi stomped off to the swamp to practice her sneaking.

She sank into the mud until not **a smidge of fluff** could be seen. It was all going well until...

...the mud left her **softer** and **shinier** than ever.

"Fifi is having a mud bath! So that's her beauty secret!"

"Cutesy wootsy!"

"Cuddly wuddly!"

"Coochie coochie coo!"

"I am NOT cute. I`m DANGEROUS!" Fifi snapped.

This was **the last straw.**

Fifi waited until her sisters were

sleeping like logs, then she ran away.

But no matter where she went...

...her problem followed.

Birds **flocked** to her.

Deer **fawned** over her.

And snakes wanted to **squeeze** her.

"Cutesy wootsy!"   "Cuddly wuddly!"   "Coochie coochie coo!"

"I am **NOT** cute. I'm..." Fifi let out a huge sigh.

"Oh, never mind."

As the animals **cooed** and *fussed* over her,
Fifi tried to look on the bright side.

"It is nice to be cuddled," she mused. "And I've made new friends already. Friends of every size, shape, color and...

Fifi **batted** her eyelashes, **puffed** up her fluff... and invited them all for a sleepover.

Fifi's sisters gaped open-mouthed as she paraded past.

"You were right!" Fifi said.

"I **AM** cute...

...DANGEROUSLY CUTE!"